The BOB~A~LONG BUNNIES
⬦— AT OAK TREE SCHOOL —⬦

The Bob-a-Long Bunnies' new home was much larger than their old one. There was a large burrow, like a sitting room, and off it ran several tunnels leading to smaller burrows, which were the bedrooms. Barty and Blossom each had their own burrow and Blossom had hung her straw hats and necklaces on the tree roots that poked through the walls. Barty hadn't anything in his, apart from his bed, but he planned to fill it later with magical things.

The morning after the bunnies moved into their new home Blossom and Barty asked if they could go outside to explore. Mrs. Bob-a-Long was busy spring-cleaning and glad to get them out from under her feet.

"Don't forget that your father said you were not to go into the forest, not until you know the paths better," she reminded them. Barty and Blossom nodded and hurried along the tunnel that led to a hole in the ground above, where they popped out their heads.

Although the old oak was deep in the heart of the forest, the other trees had stopped growing a little way away from it to form a lovely, sunny clearing where flowers grew and a brook burbled away happily.

"Don't fall in," teased Blossom, reminding Barty of the time he fell into the river near his old home. To show that he wasn't afraid, he hopped over to the brook, tripped on a stone and just saved himself from another wetting. He lay on his stomach listening to his sister's giggles until they faded away and he knew she had gone off to explore on her own.

Barty was glad to be alone. He wanted some time to himself to think about Edwin, the elf he had met in the forest the day before, and how he was going to find him again. But the sun was warm and Barty felt so comfortable that his eyes began to close and thinking became dreaming.

He dreamed that he was in the forest and that Edwin kept popping out from behind bushes and trees and disappearing again. When Barty awoke he knew he just had to go back into the forest to look for the elf and so, forgetting his father's words, he jumped up and headed for the trees.

At first he didn't venture too far into the forest as he was afraid of getting lost, but when he could find no sign of the elf he had no choice but to go a little further.

"Edwin," he called. "Edwin, it's me, Barty Bob-a-Long. If you're there, won't you please answer?"

"What are you doing here?" said a voice that made Barty almost jump right out of his skin. He swung round, hoping to see the elf but found himself looking into the angry face of his father. Barty was in serious trouble.

Back home, his ears hanging down in shame, Barty listened as his father told him off for disobeying instructions. By the time Mr. Bob-a-Long had finished with him he was beginning to think that he never wanted to see an elf again as long as he lived.

"The reason I came looking for you," said Mr. Bob-a-Long, not sounding quite so cross, "was to tell you that I had some news for you and Blossom. This morning I enrolled the two of you at Professor Bounder's Oak Tree School. You start tomorrow."

Next day, with well brushed fur and nice clean

whiskers, Blossom and Barty were ready for their day at school. Mrs. Bob-a-Long gave them their lunch, wrapped in a large dock leaf, and sent them scrambling up the tunnel into the sunlight.

Professor Bounder's classes were held on the other side of the oak tree's enormous trunk and when Barty and Blossom arrived several bunnies, some squirrels and couple of wood mice were there already. They stopped talking and playing pat-a-paw to watch the two Bob-a-Longs shyly take their places and to snigger at Barty falling over a wood mouse. But the next minute everyone was quiet and sitting up straight; for Professor Bounder had arrived.

He was a stern looking bunny with greying fur and he carried a stick which he used to point at the pupils when he wanted them to answer a question or tap them on the ears when they weren't paying attention. Barty and Blossom spent the morning learning to count up to five, at least Blossom did; Barty only got as far as two and then his thoughts wandered and he had his ears tapped by Professor Bounder.

At break time Blossom made friends with a girl bunny called Flora Furrypaws who knew where to find the best flowers for trimming hats and making necklaces. Barty kept to himself. He didn't much like school and couldn't have cared less how many carrots made five. All Barty wanted to learn about was fairies and wizards and magic.

After break Barty had his ears tapped twice more for dozing during class and was about to nod off again when something hitting him on the head made him look up. What he saw made his eyes open wide, for sitting on a branch grinning down at him was Edwin the elf. Barty watched as the troublesome creature tossed another acorn at the Professor. He swung round and glared at Barty.

"Was that you, Bob-a-Long?" he asked, rubbing his neck.

"No sir," said Barty, his innocent eyes ready to brim over with tears. Although strict, Professor Bounder had a soft heart and in all his years of teaching he had never made a pupil cry.

"Very well then," he muttered, doubtfully, "but... er... see that it doesn't happen again," and he hastily returned to the lesson.

The afternoon was to be spent on a nature walk and, true to his name, the Professor bounded through the forest with his class sometimes struggling to keep up.

"Don't dawdle! Don't dawdle!" he called to them.

More interested in pixies and elves than plants and leaves, Barty ambled along peering into shadows hoping to find something magic. It wasn't long before the other animals had disappeared out of sight.

While Barty was wondering whether to go on or to go back, a funny noise reached his ears. "Ooh! Ouch! Grr! Yow!" it went. He thought it might be one of his classmates in trouble so he hurried off to help. But it wasn't a bunny or a squirrel that he found tangled up in a bramble bush making a terrible fuss, it was Edwin. When the elf spotted Barty he yelled, "don't just stand there with your mouth open, you stupid bunny, help me out!"

But Barty wasn't feeling very friendly towards the elf, not after that episode with the acorn, and instead of lending a paw he simply said, "why should I?"

Edwin was astonished. He thought the bunny would do anything he asked. "Er... er... because I helped you find your way home the other day when you were lost."

"No you didn't," argued Barty, "my sister said she laid the trail of bluebells that led me through the forest."

"And who do you think made her put those bluebells there?" Edwin retorted. "I told you, magic isn't all flashes of light and disappearing in a puff of smoke."

Barty looked confused and Edwin could tell that he was winning him over, but then he got a bit too clever for his own good.

"And what about this morning, I gave you a good laugh when I hit that old Professor with the acorn, didn't I?"

"That wasn't funny. I nearly got into trouble for that," said Barty. "You know I think I'd be better off leaving you exactly where you are," and he started hopping away.

Edwin looked worried. He was covered in scratches, his clothes were in tatters and every time he struggled the  brambles held him more tightly. The only way out of that bush was with Barty's help and he would somehow have to coax the bunny back.